ACROSS THE POND

MICHAEL McCORMICK

With a foreword by Ron Kovic, author of *Born on the Fourth of July*

Across the Pond

Michael McCormick

Dedicated To the veterans of the Vietnam era

For CAROLYN

MICHAEL

9/23/2017

Contents

Foreword

When we thought we had read all the books about Vietnam, and had heard all the stories there were to be told, suddenly, Michael McCormick's *Across the Pond* appears and we find ourselves startled and deeply shaken by its emotional intensity. This little book with its seemingly simple yet deeply compelling narrative grips the reader from the very beginning and does not let go. It is written with the violence and fury of Leon Uris's *Battle Cry*, and the tenderness and compassion of a simple poet.

Across the Pond is more than just another book to come out of the Vietnam war. It is a poignant reminder that many of the stories of that war are yet to be told. I believe it will be recognized as one of the important books to come out of that war and McCormick will rank with the other writers of his generation, equaling their intensity, integrity, and impact. Like a stone thrown into a pond that sends out a ripple, reaching places and people not at first thought possible, *Across the Pond* does just that; with a simple, yet eloquent narrative, it becomes much greater than itself and that ripple will be felt for years to come.

With this work, McCormick takes his place among the other important chroniclers of this period. He reminds us that these stories are still out there, needing to be told, needing to be listened to and remembered. Each and every one of these stories adds up to a greater understanding of the time we have all passed through. It is our common history and will remain so forever.

This beautiful little book should be required reading in every high school, along with the other books of the Vietnam war. Because of it's brevity, stature, and dignity, I am confident *Across the Pond* will last.

Against overwhelming odds, Michael McCormick has succeeded. He has honored his country and himself with his contribution, which is simply written with great feeling. Like Erich Maria Remarque's Paul in *All Quiet on the Western Front* and Steven Crane's Henry Fleming in *The Red Badge of Courage*, his character, Sean McBride (Mac), permits us to feel what it was like to be there, day in and day out, in that place which will forever remain seared in the consciouness of a generation of Americans. So few enlisted men from that war were able to tell their stories. McCormick and very few others give a direct report from the daily existence of the infantry and grunts of that war. He puts you right there and makes you live and feel and sweat and cry, so that decades from now a generation of men and women not even born will be able to understand.

When it seemed all the other voices were still and all the stories had been told, former marine sergeant and Silver Star recipient Michael McCormick, from Jackson, Ohio, suddenly and powerfully reminds us that those voices and stories are still out there. His courageous contribution helps all of us to understand even more the great picture that was our time, the intricate and complex tapestry that was our generation. Mr. McCormick makes us wonder how many others like himself are still out there in that wilderness that so few of our generation's artists and authors have been able to escape from. Michael McCormick has not only freed himself from that bleak and dark time (that would be enough to celebrate); he has arrived as an important author and writer and he should be listened to.

With an emotional intensity that is sometimes overwhelming, *Across the Pond* is a short, violent, extremely powerful forty-two-page ride through hell that you will never forget.

Ron Kovic

Chapter I

Sean McBride, or Mac, as he was called in Vietnam, had a very bad feeling about this patrol. The company moved through the rice paddies and villages all morning with no enemy contact, but everyone felt the Vietcong were there, someplace. It was a very hot day, and most of the marines had already used up their water. The captain stopped the patrol for a rest at the edge of a village near a well. Some of the marines were beginning to gather at the well, filling their canteens. The area was surrounded by hills, and Mac knew what the Vietcong could do with a mortar. His men pulled out canteens and headed for the water as the Willie Peter round came whistling in and landed near a group of young marines.

Men screamed as the white-hot phosphorus seared through their uniforms and burned into their flesh. They heard the high-explosive rounds being dropped into the mortar tube. Everyone dove for cover. The air was filled with singing steel and death.

Mac was as close to the ground as he could get, but he still felt vulnerable and scared. He wished he could somehow make himself invisible or burrow under the ground and hide. Then he heard his friend.

"Help me, Mac. Oh God, please, someone help me. I'm hit and I can't see."

Mac did not want to look up, much less move. The mortars would be coming again, soon. He didn't want to die. *Where are your guts, man? Your friend is hurt. You know he is there, but you're scared, lying here on your belly like a worm with your face in the mud.*

Then, to his own amazement, Mac was up, running through the exploding shells to his wounded friend. *So this is what it feels like to die*, Mac thought as he reached the wounded boy and knelt down beside him.

"Don't worry, Utah. I'm going to get you out of here."

As he spoke, Mac noticed the boy's body was completely riddled with shrapnel wounds. There was blood flowing from the holes where his eyes had been.

"I can't see, Mac."

"You're going to be okay, man."

The mortars stopped crashing in, but Mac could hear more shells plunking into the mortar tube. *Damn, they're good with that thing—and fast*, he thought. As the next barrage of mortars began to explode around them, Mac grabbed the wounded boy and started dragging him to cover. They reached a ditch, and Mac shoved the kid in and fell on top of him. The ground shook above their heads. Mac reached down and felt the boy's neck for a pulse. There was none.

Chapter II

Mac lurched forward violently, suddenly awakened from the nightmare he had been having for months. He was sweating and shivering at the same time.

When he first arrived in Vietnam, Mac had been assigned to Zang's squad. Zang had a reputation as a very tough squad leader. He was completing his second tour of duty in Vietnam and was somewhat crazy. The squad was patrolling near An Hoa, South Vietnam, when they started taking sniper fire from a village they were passing. The marines hit the deck and returned fire. After a few minutes, the firing stopped. The men prepared to continue the patrol. They knew the sniper had probably made his escape through a nearby tunnel.

"Form up on-line; we're going to sweep through the vill and try to flush out that sniper," Zang said.

At this time, Mac had not been in Vietnam long, but he had been there long enough to know the sniper was gone. It seemed foolish to delay the patrol because of one sniper, who was probably gone anyway. Then Mac heard Zang say something about execution call. Mac knew Zang was from Chicago. He had boasted about having connections with the Mafia. He wanted to become a lieutenant in the mob when he got back to the world.

The squad got on-line and swept through the village. They did not receive any enemy fire. The people in the village had taken cover in underground bunkers. Zang had his men search the bunkers and bring all the people to the center of the village. There were approximately fifty Vietnamese in the bunker complex: old men, women, and children. The exceptions were three young men, who appeared to be about seventeen years old. Zang pulled the young men off to the side. He was in a rage.

Zang pointed at the young men and said, "You VC."

The boys shook their heads violently. "No VC! No VC!"

Mac could see the fear in their eyes. The marines towered over the diminutive Vietnamese, and the marines were dirty, sweaty, tired, hungry, and not very happy about having just been shot at, but Mac didn't think Zang would actually do anything to the young men. He thought Zang was trying to scare them, possibly to find out where the Vietcong were. But Zang pulled his pistol out of its holster, cocked it, and put the barrel against the head of the oldest Vietnamese boy. Zang was red in the face, hyperventilating. He was very angry.

"You're VC, and I'm going to kill you if you don't tell me where your unit is."

Mac was worried; he could see that Zang meant business. He walked over to Zang and stood next to him. "This isn't right, man," Mac said. "I don't think they even understand what you're saying."

"Shut up and get back where you belong," Zang barked. "These fucking gooks damn well know what I'm saying, and if they don't tell me where their Vietcong unit is, we're going to have an execution call."

Mac could not believe it. What was he going to do, he thought, get into a firefight with his squad leader?

Zang lowered the pistol, grabbed the collar of the boy, and pulled him closer. He pointed the pistol directly at the boy's heart.

"No!" Mac said.

Zang squeezed the trigger. The bullet struck the Vietnamese in the chest, sending blood spurting through the air. The boy crumpled to the ground, dead. The villagers gathered around the body, crying. The boy's mother cradled his body in her arms, sobbing. The village men stood motionless. There was fear and hatred in their eyes.

"You're crazy, Zang," Mac said.

Zang cocked the pistol again and pointed it at Mac's head. "What did you say, mister?"

"Go to hell!" Mac said, then turned and walked away.

Chapter III

The Alamo wasn't really a fort at all. Evidently, there had been an American outpost there at one time, halfway between An Hoa and Phu Loc VI. The entire area was now heavily booby-trapped and the Vietcong liked to mine the road and snipe at the marines. Mac's squad was assigned to the job of flank security. He and his squad were moving along the sides of the road, one fire team on each side, providing security for the main body of marines sweeping the road for mines. When he heard the explosion, Mac hit the deck hard, a reflex that required no conscious thought. One learned fast in this environment that your life often depended on how fast you could duck. The blast had been on the other side of the road. Mac became aware that he was lying on the ground with his face in the dirt. He felt afraid, then embarrassed that he was hugging the ground. Mac rose to his feet quickly and glanced around to see if his men had sensed his fear. They were all still lying facedown in the mud. He ran across the road and along the rice paddy dike to the downed marine. It was one of the new men, Chris, from Nebraska.

"How you doing, Chris?"

"I think I tripped a frag, Mac. I heard the spoon fly."

"Don't worry, man; the choppers are on the way."

The wounds were not bad. Chris caught some shrapnel from a Chi Com grenade booby trap in the legs. He would be going to Da Nang and then to a hospital in Japan. A corpsman appeared and began placing battle dressings on the boy's wounds. A medivac chopper arrived. Mac and three other marines put Chris on a poncho and carried him to the bird.

The patrol moved out. Ten minutes later another explosion shook the ground. The truck following the road sweep hit a mine. The blast was so powerful, it flipped the truck over on its side, killing both marines inside. Pieces of metal, rubber, and dirt rained down. The marines put what they could find of the two men in a poncho and called another medivac.

It was decided that Mac's platoon would patrol the area around the Alamo and try to make contact with the enemy unit that had planted the mine. The patrol moved out, the column snaking its way through the rice paddies, along the dikes, and past the villages. After ten minutes of patrolling, the point man tripped a booby trap. The bomb had been made from an American artillery round that had not exploded. The Vietcong rigged up the shell to explode when a wire was tripped, using a friction device. The marine who tripped the explosive was blown to pieces. The four marines behind him were all seriously wounded. One kid lost both of his legs at the thigh and, in a state of shock, was trying to get up and walk on the stumps. Another boy lost a leg, an arm, and an eye. He was lying on his back, crying out for his mother.

After the dead and wounded had been flown out, the rest of the marines moved out. Thirty minutes later, another booby trap exploded. There were more dead and wounded. Calls went out for "Corpsman, up!" A medic jumped up and ran in the direction of the wounded. He stepped on a booby trap and was killed instantly. Marines bandaged marines and the helicopters were called. When the birds landed, four marines carrying a wounded boy in a poncho tripped a booby trap and were themselves wounded. A third medivac chopper landed on a mine, wounding the pilot. The carnage continued throughout the day. The marines would move out, get blown up, call in the choppers, and get blown up again. Not one enemy soldier was spotted during this time.

Mac's squad took point. They hadn't gone very far when the platoon leader got on the radio.

"Hotel Two Bravo, Hotel Two Bravo, this is Hotel Two, over."

"Hotel Two, this is Two Bravo, over," Mac said into the handset.

"Mac, find us a spot to bed down for the night, over."

"Understand, Two," Mac said.

A suitable location for a night defensive perimeter was found, and the men started digging in for the night. The next day was more of the same. The area was so heavily booby-trapped, the marines could not move fifty yards without tripping an explosion.

Some of the men reached their breaking point. The marines had volunteered to fight, not get blown up, day after day, with no enemy contact. The morning of the third day near the Alamo, Mac was approached by two of his fellow squad leaders.

"Mac, we're taking our men out of here."

"Where you going to go?" Mac responded.

"Back to the fire base."

"I don't think that's the answer," Mac said.

The rogue marines formed up in a column, the two squad leaders at the head. They began walking toward the perimeter. Sergeant Milner was watching. He walked over to the two leaders.

"Where are you going, corporal?

"The men can't take any more, sergeant. I'm taking them back to An Hoa."

The sergeant drew his pistol and chambered a round.

"You're not going anywhere, marine. If anyone tries to leave this perimeter without orders, I'll shoot him myself. Now get these people back to their positions."

The rebel marines hung their heads and went back to their fighting holes.

The platoon patrolled near the Alamo for two more days; then they were flown back to An Hoa for hot chow, showers, and mail. The mutiny was never mentioned again.

Chapter IV

Darkness began to envelop the fire base at Phu Loc VI. The marines of Mac's squad inspected their gear, checked weapons, counted grenades, and distributed ammunition. They darkened their faces and joked back and forth to cut the tension. When it was dark, Mac led his men to the ambush site. He took the long way around, avoiding any roads or trails. Mac didn't want to get his squad killed before they could get into position. The marines walked through the rice paddies and worked their way back to the road, nearly a mile south of the fire base entrance. Mac located the spot he had picked out during the day patrol and set in his men. They faced the road from a small hill about thirty yards away, with a clear field of fire in all directions.

Mac positioned his machine-gun team in the center of the squad. A rifle fire team was on each side of the gun, with Mac and the radioman next to the gunner. When the ambush was sprung, the gun would open up first. Every third man would remain awake during the night. No one expected the Vietcong to come walking right down the road so near the marine base, but enemy movement had been spotted in the area recently.

It was 2:00 A.M. when Mac felt something on his shoulder. He was awake at once and instinctively reached for his pistol. The marine next to him was pointing down the road.

"VC."

Mac could barely see the silhouettes in the darkness. A dozen Vietcong were walking down the road, laughing and talking as they walked. Mac glanced over at his machine gunner and realized he was asleep. Mac would have to spring the ambush himself.

"Fire!" Mac yelled, as he squeezed off several pistol rounds at the Vietcong.

The firing only lasted thirty seconds, but it seemed like much longer. There was no return fire from the enemy. As a matter of fact, the Vietcong took off running when the first shot was fired. Mac waited silently, listening for sounds of movement. His radioman looked up.

"Mac, the lieutenant is on the horn."

"This is Mac, over."

"What have you got out there, Mac, over."

"Be advised we have ambushed a squad-sized enemy force coming down the road, over."

"Understand, Mac. Are there any casualties, over."

"Negative, lieutenant. Request some light over the kill zone, over."

The flares popped overhead and the marines saw several bodies lying in the road. At first light, Mac took a fire team to examine the bodies. One of the enemy dead was a woman. As Mac came closer, he noticed her long black hair. There was a bullet hole in her chest, just above the heart.

Chapter V

Sean McBride had survived his war in Vietnam. At the age of nineteen, he was about to be decorated with the Silver Star medal, the third highest military award for gallantry in action.

A voice came over the loudspeaker saying, "Ladies and gentlemen, the president of the United States takes pride in presenting the Silver Star to Corp. Sean McBride."

The young marine stood straight and tall in his dress blue uniform, the gold buttons on his chest and the blood red stripe running down the sides of his trousers reflecting the late afternoon sunlight. As he waited on the parade deck at the sprawling marine base in North Carolina, McBride remembered his friends Jimmy and Bleachman. There were several hundred people assembled to watch the ceremony, including Sean's family.

The announcer continued, "Corporal McBride's platoon was operating near Cu Lap Village in Quang Nam Province, South Vietnam, when the marines came under intense small-arms, automatic-weapon, and mortar fire from a numerically superior enemy force occupying positions on three sides of the friendly unit. Rapidly assessing the situation, Corporal McBride obtained a machine gun from a wounded marine and directed a heavy volume of suppressive fire at the enemy soldiers while his men maneuvered to a more tenable position. Continuing his determined efforts, Corporal McBride advanced across the fire-swept terrain, encountering and killing several enemy soldiers. His heroic actions and selfless devotion to duty at great personal risk inspired his beleaguered platoon and were instrumental in recovering all of its casualties while accounting for fifteen enemy dead."

McBride took a few steps forward and stopped, standing at attention. The general walked over to him, pinned the medal on his chest, and shook his hand. Sean glanced over at his family. He thought about the events that had brought him to this moment.

Chapter VI

The seventeen-year-old cowboy pulled down the brim of his Stetson hat and climbed over the gray wooden corral. He gently lowered himself onto the back of the big Brahma bull. The cowboy was lean and tough, and he moved about with the precision of a cat. A handsome young Irishman with brown hair and green eyes, he had a firm set to his jaw and a habit of looking a man in the eyes as he spoke. Sean McBride tried not to think about the bull's horns, only inches away, as he busied himself with the rigging he carefully wrapped around his hand. The rosined leather strap must be tight enough for a firm grip during the ride on the bucking bull, yet loose enough for the cowboy to pull his hand free when it was time to get off the animal. The combination had to be right, or the cowboy could get caught in the rigging and be pounded to death by the bucking, spinning bull.

"Does the rigging look okay?"

"It looks good, Son. Be careful."

Sean's father was a schoolman, an Irishman with curly black hair and a master's degree in education. He was in his late thirties and had been breaking and training horses all his life. He loved horses and tried to teach his two sons everything he knew. He didn't like these damn bulls, though. They were mean and would intentionally try to hurt, even kill, a cowboy. A horse, on the other hand, would go out of its way to avoid stepping on a downed man.

Sean adjusted his hat once more and moved his legs in closer to the sides of the bull. He became aware of a gentle breeze blowing through the tops of the trees above the rodeo arena. A hush had fallen over the crowd. He could feel the eyes of the people on him. Sean glanced around to see if his mother and girlfriend were in the crowd. They were there, about halfway up in the stands. He inspected the rigging one last time. It seemed to be the way he wanted it.

"Let's do it," he said.

Sean nodded, the bucking chute door swung open, and the bull lunged through the gate, leaping into the air, landing to the right with a jolt, then spinning to the left violently. The big Brahma continued to spin for several seconds, and the cowboy started to relax slightly and roll with the frenzied movements of the powerful animal. Sean's legs were hugging the sides of the bull and he was beginning to think he would make it to the whistle when suddenly the bull began to spin in the opposite direction. The cowboy lost his concentration for a second; the bull sensed this at the same instantand began to spin even harder. Sean was flying through the air now and in what seemed like slow motion watched the ground come up to meet him. He slammed into the arena floor, landing on his face, shoulder, and hip at the same time. Instinctively he began to scramble to his feet, but it seemed to be taking a very long time for his body to respond to the message his brain was sending to it. He was thinking he had to get over the fence before the bull had a chance to turn and come for him. He was on his hands and knees now, aware of the throbbing pain in his shoulder, when he saw a brightly colored object streak past his field of vision. *Rodeo clown*, he thought. *The clown is going to distract the bull long enough for me to make my escape over the fence.*

Sean pulled himself to his feet and was about to take a step when he felt the horns slam into the small of his back, throwing him to the ground again. He sensed the bull pass over his body as he lay motionless. The animal turned and charged again, this time picking the cowboy up with its horns and flinging him through the air. Once again Sean lay still. By this time, the clown had managed to get into position and, as the bull prepared to attack again, ran between the downed cowboy and the bull. The bull followed the clown, giving Sean a chance to get to his feet and scramble over the fence to safety.

"You all right, Son?"

"Yes, I think so. Let's go home."

Mapleview Farm sat quietly among the maple trees and rolling hills of southern Ohio. The lane cut abruptly off the main highway, winding its way lazily up the knoll past the pine trees near the cemetery and around the pond, stopping behind the white house with a red tin roof and white pillars in front. The McBride family was a close one. Everyone worked together to raise the Appaloosa and quarter horses. They also raised Black Angus cattle and had several cats, dogs, and chickens. The pond was full of bass, catfish, and bluegills. Hunting was good in this area. Deer and rabbit were taken in the winter. Squirrel was hunted in the fall.

Polly McBride was a pretty woman with brown hair and eyes. Her family was her life. She kept her home clean and bright and was always there for her family. She loved to work in her garden in summer and cook and can foods in winter.

Patrick was the youngest son; at sixteen he was a year younger than Sean. The two boys had played and worked together all their lives. They loved each other, but they still fought.

One afternoon, the father decided to break one of the young horses he had agreed to train. Four fillies had been roped off the range in Colorado and shipped east for sale. None of the young horses had ever been touched by humans. With the help of a bucket of grain and a lasso, one of the fillies, a big bay, was brought along to the breaking corral, where a twitch was applied to her lower lip. Then the breaking saddle and a bridle were gently placed on the animal.

"I'll go first, Dad, and wear her down for Sean," Patrick said.

The three men looked at each others' faces, aware of the danger, but it was not discussed. Sean moved around to the other side of the horse and placed his hand on her neck. The father stood on the opposite side. Patrick slipped into the saddle and nodded his head.

It took a second for the filly to realize she was free; then she shot straight up in the air, landing on all four extended legs with a jolt. Then she started to buck frantically down the hill. She reared up on her hind legs, striking the air with her hooves. The young cowboy held his balance, but the filly was determined to lose her rider and became even more enraged, cutting to the left, then back to the right. Patrick could not stay with her. He went over her withers into the grass. The father hurried over to his youngest son.

"You okay, Son?"

"Yes, I'm fine."

"I want to try her," Sean said.

The men caught the filly, and Sean prepared to take his turn in the saddle. He climbed on the filly and she immediately reared into the air again, striking at the men, then bucking with all her strength, nearly falling into a fence. Sean was thrown from the horse, landing near the spot where his brother had gone down.

"You hurt, Son?"

"No, Dad."

"I want to try her again," Patrick said.

He got on the filly and this time stayed with her a long time. She began to tire, calming some, then stopped bucking and went into a lope, then a trot, and finally walked around the corral.

"I'm proud of you boys; you've bucked her out."

Chapter VII

The Vietnam War was rumbling in a distant land across the sea. Sean McBride was about to graduate from high school. He had decided not to attend the university next fall. High school had been much like jail for him.

The marine recruiter swaggered onto the stage of Sean's high school auditorium. He stood ramrod straight in his dress blues, talking about God and country, invoking the memory of John F. Kennedy, who had said, "Ask not what your country can do for you; ask what you can do for your country."

The marines had always held special significance for Sean McBride. He had grown up listening to stories about the incredibly brave marines of World War II. The marines were heroes to Sean's father and to other men Sean looked up to. In Sean's mind, the marines were legends, bigger than life. They had helped save us from Fascism and tyranny at places like Iwo Jima, Guadalcanal, and Okinawa. Sean realized that it was his destiny to become one of these marines. He knew this meant he would be going to war in Vietnam. He didn't understand the war and hadn't even thought about it much. In his youthful enthusiasm and political naïveté, he accepted what he was taught in school and trusted his leaders. Sean was being told by the media that the majority of the American people were in favor of the war in Vietnam. Considerable subtle pressure was being put on him to join the fight. Sean was about to make one of the most important decisions of his life, at a very early age, with virtually no factual information available to him. He would not learn for many years that the American generals in Vietnam had lied to the politicians in Washington and that they in turn had lied to the people. Sean's father, uncles, indeed, every man he respected and trusted had gone to war.

After school, Sean found his girlfriend, Christy, at cheerleading practice. He told her he wanted to talk. She offered to give him a ride home in her mother's car. They stepped outside. It was winter and the ice-cold wind took away their breath. There was a foot of new snow glistening in the lights around the gymnasium, and more falling heavily. Sean and Christy had been going steady for two years. She wore his class ring on her finger wrapped in Angora thread. Christy was a beautiful young girl, petite, with black hair and blue eyes. She was one of the most popular girls in school. They got into the car and drove past the football field and out Highway 139 toward the McBride home.

"I've made a decision," Sean said.

Christy looked at his face, searching.

"I've decided to join the marines."

She was frightened and began to tremble slightly.

"That means you'll have to go to Vietnam. Sean, I love you. I don't want you to go away."

"I love you, too, but this is something I feel I have to do. I don't understand it really, but I know I'd never be able to live with myself if I didn't go."

"It's not our stupid war," she said. "We could get married, and you could get a deferment."

"I won't; you know that."

"Yes, I suppose I do. I guess I've always known that about you."

They drove along silently the rest of the way. The heavy snow muffled all sound and made the silence even more difficult.

Christy dropped Sean off in front of his house and left. He walked inside and was greeted by the aroma of food cooking. The dinner table was set, and there was a fire in the living room fireplace.

"Hi, Mom," Sean said, giving his mother a kiss on the cheek as he grabbed a carrot from the table.

"Was that Christy?"

"Yes. She had to get home."

"Wake your father and tell Patrick dinner is ready."

Sean went into the living room and nudged his father awake. He had fallen asleep in his red reclining chair reading the newspaper.

"Dad, dinner's ready."

Sean looked around the living room he had helped his father and grandfather build. He was proud of the pine walls and hardwood floors they had worked so hard to build. There were rows of books along one wall, and a picture of the Snake River hung over the sofa. Sean went up the wooden staircase to the bedroom he and his brother shared.

"It's time for dinner!" he called.

Looking at the bunk beds he and Patrick had slept in since they were small boys, Sean realized for the first time that things would be different now. He was no longer a boy.

The family settled into the kitchen for dinner. They sat at the wooden table covered with a white tablecloth and began to eat the roast beef, mashed potatoes and gravy, vegetables, fruit, and milk.

"I've made a decision," Sean said. "I want to join the marines."

Sean's mother nearly dropped her fork. His father looked shocked, concerned, then proud. Patrick had a puzzled look on his face.

"Why the marines, Son?"

"I want to make a contribution. We're at war and I think the marines are the best."

Sean's mother started to cry. She got up and left the table. Patrick looked even more perplexed.

"I think it's admirable that you want to do your part, Son, but have you considered the Air Force or the navy?"

"No, I haven't. I've made my choice."

"Well, Son, if that's what you want."

Chapter VIII

The bus pulled into the dreary-looking Marine Corps recruit depot at Parris Island, South Carolina. It was about three O'clock in the morning. Most of the young men on board were asleep when it came to a halt. A sergeant wearing a "Smokey the Bear" hat climbed on.

"Welcome to PI, gentlemen. The Marine Corps hopes you enjoy your stay here. Now you people have ten seconds to get the fuck off this bus and fall in on the little yellow footprints. Move! Move! Move!"

The sergeant then grabbed the two boys closest to him and pushed them out the door. The recruits formed up on the footprints and were herded into a large gray building with a long row of barber chairs in the center. A marine in a fresh, clean uniform stood behind each chair with clippers in his hands, grinning. Sean sat in one of the chairs.

"Just take a little off the sides," Sean said, joking nervously.

"Right," the corporal said, as he began shaving off all of Sean's hair.

The recruits were taken to another building where they were told to strip, given shots, and directed to deposit all their clothing and personal possessions into canvas bags. Anything related to their civilian life, hair, clothes, rings, was being systematically discarded. The recruits were then issued seabags, uniforms, and other military gear. Stripped of their hair and belongings, everyone now looked the same. The process of becoming a marine had begun.

The rest of the day, the recruits would hurry up and wait. They double-timed from one location to the next, only to wait, at attention, to be issued a piece of gear. Late that night, they were allowed to sleep.

The following morning, the recruits were awakened at four to the sound of metal trash cans being thrown to the hardwood floors. Every light in the squad bay was on, and all the drill instructors were running through the building upsetting bunks with men in them.

"Get up! Get up! Get up! Drop your cocks and grab your socks. Reveille! Reveille!" they yelled.

The drill instructors continued to train the recruits. They were taught to clean their gear, stand at attention, and wear uniforms properly. Individual egos were broken down. Teamwork was stressed above all else. When an individual made a mistake, the entire platoon was punished. The bodies of the young recruits became leaner and harder. At lunch, the drill instructors would say, "Well, ladies, today we are having duck for lunch. We're going to duck into the mess hall and duck out again."

The drill instructors called the recruits scumbags, girls, and ladies. They liked to say things like: "You people are not even marines and you're not civilians either. What you are is recruits, and recruits are lower than whale shit, and whale shit is on the bottom of the ocean."

Another thing the drill instructors liked to do was have the platoon hold up their rifles and chant, "This is my rifle; it is my life. I love my rifle; in combat, without it I will surely die."

The recruits stood in the hot, sweltering sun for hour upon hour, at times with their arms outstretched and their rifles placed across the tops of their hands. Some of them passed out, only to be left where they dropped.

On one extremely hot day in July, as the platoon was marching, one of the young recruits broke formation and went berserk. He fell to the ground and pounded it with his fists, crying, "I can't take it anymore!"

A small white truck with a red cross on the side arrived a few minutes later. Two men in white jackets got out, put a strait-jacket on the recruit, and took him away.

During the final phase of basic training, the recruits were taught how to kill up close. They learned to use anything available to kill the enemy, a knife, a bayonet, or even bare hands if necessary. It was clear to the recruits that their days of youthful innocence were over. They were going to war, and war was not a pretty business.

To make sure the recruits understood, the senior drill instructor told the platoon, "Take a look around you, men. If you have learned your lessons well, only a quarter of this platoon will come home from Vietnam in a box. Another quarter will live in wheelchairs for the rest of their lives. God help you."

The sun was setting on the day before graduation. The platoon was putting the finishing touches on its marching skills. Everyone had orders for Westpac, Vietnam. The DI began to sing cadence, and the platoon answered back.

"Hey there, Marine."
"Hey there, Marine."
"Now where you going?"
"Now where you going?"
"Going across the pond."

"Going across the pond."

"Going to fight the Cong."

"Going to fight the Cong."

"So if you die."

"So if you die."

"Before I do."

"Before I do."

"Won't cha tell Saint Peter."

"Won't cha tell Saint Peter."

"I'm comin', too."

"I'm comin', too."

Chapter IX

The marines of Hue had no way of knowing the enemy Tet offensive of 1968 would be the turning point of the war in Vietnam. The Americans would win the battle, but the Vietcong and the North Vietnamese Army (NVA) would claim a psychological victory. It was the beginning of the end of the war.

Vietnam was not a popular war. If it had been like the participation in World War II, Hue would still be a popular name. The marines who fought there and survived would now be heroes. Young Americans who died there would be remembered. Instead, the marines who fought in Vietnam returned to a nation that had turned its back on them. The United States would be unable to separate the war from the warrior. America would disgrace itself by scapegoating the very young men it had sent to fight. The sacrifices made and the hardships endured by those who faced the brutal month-long house-to-house fighting would go unnoticed next to the headlines about returning veterans going off and shooting up the town.

In Hue, two understrength marine battalions fought eight enemy battalions.

The truck convoy neared Hue. The marines watched in horror as the Vietnamese civilians streamed out of the city and down Highway 1 on foot by the thousands, carrying whatever belongings they could hold.

The enemy troops attacked the marine convoy just inside Hue. North Vietnamese soldiers took positions in a graveyard. They detonated a mine as the lead truck passed over it. Twenty marines were killed or wounded in that truck. Pieces of their young bodies were strewn all over the road.

Mac and his machine-gun team took cover behind the gravestones in the cemetery and began returning fire. Another truck came up and started shooting fifty-caliber machine guns, blowing away the paddy dikes and grave mounds concealing the North Vietnamese soldiers. As the dirt walls began to disintegrate, the enemy panicked and ran into the open. Mac and his machine-gun team cut them down. The battle ended when the NVA retreated under cover of smoke.

February was monsoon season in Vietnam. It was cold, wet, and dreary in Hue. During the early days of the fighting marines died trying to cross streets and move through doors. The enemy knew where the marines would cross and would be waiting for them with machine guns. The young marines ran into a wall of bullets. Crossing a street became a deadly business. A marine would be wounded or killed in the street, and his body would lie there until his buddies went out into the street to get him. Often another marine would be hit in the process and more marines would have to run into the withering machine-gun fire again. Many marines were lost in this manner, because the marines refused to leave one dead or wounded comrade behind. Eventually, the marines began blowing holes through walls with a recoilless rifle, and casualties became much lighter.

Bodies of dead enemy soldiers were lying in the streets. Their bloated, stinking bodies were strangely contorted, with arms outstretched and their legs and heads blown off.

Two weeks into the fighting, a marine chaplain arrived in Hue. There was a ceremony held for the dead marines.

Several rows of rifles with fixed bayonets were stuck in the ground. Helmets of dead marines were placed on the rifle butts. The chaplain said the young marines had not died in vain. He said God was on their side. Mac and the marines of Hotel Company paused for a moment to imagine what hell would look like if this was God's work. Many of the marines in Hue were taking on the thousand-yard stare. It is a vacant, distant, frightened, exhausted look that those who have been in combat for long periods of time with no sleep and little water would recognize. The next morning, an enemy sniper tried to kill Mac as he crossed the street. Mac realized that he was too tired, cold, and hungry to even care. There was a person out there he didn't even know, and that person was trying to kill him. Mac felt an eerie, surrealistic rush of emotion that left him ashamed to be part of such madness.

The next morning, Hotel Company advanced to a row of houses that had to be secured. Mac and his squad entered a house and were told to wait. As he stood looking out the window, Mac saw a Vietnamese soldier wearing a pith helmet walk past with his rifle slung over his shoulder. The enemy lines were farther up, and Mac thought this was not an enemy soldier. Then he understood the mistake that could have cost him his life: only enemy soldiers wore the white pith helmets. Mac had just seen an enemy soldier stroll past the window like he had all day. Fortunately for Mac, the enemy had not seen him or he wouldn't still be thinking about it. Mac thought it was very unlikely that the enemy soldier would return, but he would be ready just in case. He rested his M-16 rifle on the windowsill and moved the selector to single fire. A minute later, the same soldier returned. He was very close and this time he held his rifle in his hands and crouched low. He turned and looked at Mac. Both soldiers froze for an instant. Then the enemy started to raise his weapon. Mac squeezed the trigger and felt the rifle gently buck against his shoulder. The round slammed into the enemy soldier's chest. The man looked surprised, then grimaced in pain as the force of the bullet knocked him down. He was dead.

The next morning, Hotel Company moved out early. The patrol came upon four enemy officers in a hooch with several women. Grenades were tossed in the windows. Two marines went inside. One of the women and one of the enemy officers were alive, but they were all blown up. Two pistol shots echoed through the streets.

The brutal, bloody, house-to-house, street-to-street slaughter went on for thirty more days in Hue.

Near the end of the battle, Hotel Company pursued a fleeing unit of enemy soldiers into the nearby hills. The marine patrol reached the base of a hill that was covered with brush and trees. The enemy was holed up inside two old block buildings at the top of the hill. They opened up with machine guns, pinning down the marines. The captain got on the radio and called for air strikes on the enemy positions. There was another marine company nearby, so instead of directing the jet bombing run parallel to the front line, he brought them in overhead, thus cutting down the chances of overshooting the target and bombing the other company. The U.S. Air Force jet came in low and dropped napalm canisters on the hilltop. The enemy fire ceased.

The captain stood up to get a better look. The enemy position was smoking and burning from a direct hit. Standing with his radio, the captain brought the aircraft in for another air strike. The jet banked around and came shrieking in low over the treetops, releasing four 500-pound bombs. There was a tremendous roar, and Mac was slammed to the ground by a huge concussion. He knew two of the bombs had exploded behind him. The pilot had pressed the button a second too soon. The grunts staggered around for a few moments trying to comprehend what had happened. Some of the marines were calling for corpsmen. Then they found four young marines, blown apart, arms and legs and intestines and brains smeared in the bushes. It was a direct hit. Marines were getting sick, turning away, not wanting to look at the mess. Mac and another marine put what was left of the kids in ponchos. Fox Company moved up to secure the hill. They found twenty-two enemy dead in the demolished blockhouses. It didn't seem to matter much to the marines of Hotel Company.

Chapter X

After Hue, Hotel Company went back to patrolling near An Hoa. A large enemy unit had been spotted near the fire base. Hotel Company would try to find the enemy and engage them in battle. Mac had just finished his meal of C rations, instant coffee, cheese, and crackers when the first wave of helicopters landed.

Mac was an infantry squad leader now. He had fought in Hue and survived. There was no information on the landing zone, so the marines assumed it would be hot. Mac and his men filed onto the choppers and sat down. Knots formed in their stomachs. Mouths were dry. Men avoided making eye contact because they were afraid and didn't want the other men to know. The birds lifted off and it was quiet except for the thumping of rotor blades. Each man was alone with his thoughts.

After forty minutes in the air, the choppers began their descent. The marines braced for the bullets that might come ripping through the hulls of the helicopters. The choppers touched down, and the ramp door came down. Men jumped to their feet and ran down the ramp into the landing zone. Mac burst out of the chopper, and his legs were churning into the sunlight. He relaxed a little when he realized there was no incoming enemy fire. A hasty perimeter was set up around the helicopters until they left. Then the company formed up in a column and moved out.

As he walked, Mac thought about his new radioman, Jimmy. He was a good-looking kid from New York, with black hair and dark eyes. Jimmy was nineteen years old and new to the squad but had already proven himself to be a very adept radioman. Mac had a bad feeling about this kid. For some reason he sensed Jimmy was not going to make it. There was no way Mac could predict who would live and who would die, but he had this feeling. *Got to keep an eye on that kid*, Mac said to himself. He was also thinking about Bleachman, who was short. Bleachman was due to go home soon, and he was getting sloppy. That was dangerous. Bleachman was from South Philadelphia. He was a homely man with a pockmarked face and stringy hair, but he had been a good marine and squad leader.

Hotel Company patrolled through the villages and rice paddies all morning with no enemy contact. The captain called for a rest break. Marines spread out and opened canteens and cigarettes. Mac noticed a young-looking marine from another platoon wandering around. He told the kid to get back to his squad. There could be booby traps. The company moved out. There was an explosion. Mac moved up the column and found the boy he had just been talking with. The kid was lying on his back, hands over his face. He had stepped off the trail and grabbed a vine running up the bank. The vine was booby-trapped, and the blast hit the boy in the face. Mac got to the kid first. He knelt down and cradled the boy's head in his arm. The boy was coughing blood and trying to speak, but too much of his face was gone.

"Medic! Corpsman, up! Corpsman, up!"

It was too late. The young marine convulsed and died. A helicopter came and took away the body. Hotel Company moved out.

About an hour later, someone spotted enemy soldiers running across a clearing. The captain decided to sweep through the area with a platoon on-line, followed by the rest of the company in column. Second Platoon would be the platoon on-line. Mac's Second Squad would be on the right, with First and Third squads on his left. The platoon would be sweeping through tall elephant grass, across open ground, through a tree line, and into a village. It was a great place for an ambush, and Mac knew it.

"What do you think, Bleachman?"

"I don't like it, Mac; it feels like a trap."

"Mac, I see enemy movement to our right front," Jimmy said.

"Get the lieutenant on the horn," Mac said.

"Hotel Two, Hotel Two, this is Two Bravo, over," Jimmy barked into the handset.

Jimmy handed Mac the handset.

"Hotel Two, be advised I have enemy activity on my right front, over."

"Understand, Mac, move forward, over."

Mac realized he was in serious trouble. The lieutenant and the skipper both knew it looked like a trap and they were going to march the men into it anyway. *Damn officers*, Mac thought. *We're going to get hurt bad if we do this.* The platoon moved out of the elephant grass and into the open.

Mac looked at Bleachman and was about to say something when Bleachman's head exploded. A machine-gun bullet ripped through the top of his skull, splattering pieces of bone, brain tissue, and blood on Mac's face and flak jacket. Bleachman was lying on his face. Mac knelt down to feel for a pulse and looked over at Jimmy. He was about to tell Jimmy that Bleachman was dead when he saw Jimmy take a bullet in the forehead. Jimmy was dead.

At that moment, Mac knew he was going to die. He was surprised, because he wasn't afraid. He just felt tired and angry that he was about to die in some dirt field at the age of eighteen. Mac gave the order to pull back and started dragging Bleachman's body to a small ditch just inside the elephant grass. The enemy was using mortars now, in addition to the small-arms and machine-gun fire. Mac knew his situation was not good. He had two dead and two seriously wounded out of seven. First and Third squads were taking heavy fire also. Mac knew the enemy soldiers would be trying to flank his position and come through the elephant grass. He organized his men in a small defensive perimeter and borrowed a machine gun from one of the wounded. Mac fired the gun into the tree line to his front and into the elephant grass on his right. A bullet whizzed past his ear, close. Mac turned and saw the enemy soldier running through the grass, firing as he came. Mac squeezed off a quick burst of machine-gun fire, shooting from the hip. The burst hit the enemy soldier in the chest and knocked him over backward. Mac was firing the rest of his machine-gun ammo when the mortar landed beside him. The concussion picked him up and slammed him to the ground. There was a roaring in his ears, but the shrapnel had missed. Mac located a grenade launcher and started lobbing grenades at the enemy. A second enemy soldier came running through the grass. Mac hit him with a grenade, and the soldier's body flew apart. Mac picked up a rifle with a bayonet attached and started through the elephant grass. He met an enemy soldier and tried to fire his weapon. The rifle jammed. Mac lunged at the enemy with his bayonet. The blade sliced through the soldier's shirt and into his belly. The enemy looked stunned, then scared, then in agony as the bayonet plunged deeper into his guts. Mac tried to pull the bayonet free, but it would not budge. He cleared the piece and fired a round, freeing the bayonet.

Mac returned to his squad. The fighting died down and the enemy withdrew as darkness fell.

Chapter XI

When he came home from Vietnam, Sean McBride stayed with his parents for several months. Then he became restless and decided to tour the country on his motorcycle. His hair was getting long, and he was beginning to feel like a civilian again.

Sean had been on the road for weeks when he pulled into the truck stop somewhere in the South. He was hungry and needed a shave and bath. As he filled up with gas, Sean sensed that he was being watched. There were four of them, two men and two women, standing outside the café. Sean considered moving on, but he was hungry and tired. He parked his bike and walked into the restaurant. As he passed the four people who had been staring at him, he looked them in the eyes.

"Look at the hippie," one of the men said.

"Yeah," the second man said. "I think he needs a bath."

Sean went inside, sat down, and ordered his food.

The four people followed Sean inside and took a booth near his. They continued to laugh and make insulting remarks as Sean ate. When he finished his meal, Sean walked out to his bike. He started the motorcycle and was about to leave when one of the women from the four appeared and turned off the ignition and put his keys in her pocket. The other three walked over.

"Where you going in such a hurry, boy?" said the first man.

"Yeah, weirdo, we told you we don't like longhairs and hippies in these parts. Now we're going to have to teach you a lesson," the second man said.

Sean stepped off his bike carefully. One of the men held a hand behind his back. *That's where it will come*, Sean thought. *It will be soon now.* The tire iron came around just as Sean ducked. He countered with a reverse punch to the man's throat, and the man went down on one knee, gasping for air, clutching his throat. The other man stung Sean with a right hand that opened a cut just above his eye. Sean attacked with a front kick to the groin and a roundhouse kick to the man's head. The first man, still on his knees, signaled he had had enough. Sean took his keys from the woman, started his bike, and was about to leave. Blood was streaming down his face.

A woman had been watching from inside the café. She pulled a handkerchief from her purse and came outside. Sean saw her coming and stopped. She was one of the most beautiful women he had ever seen. She had dark, mysterious eyes and long black hair. There was elegance and dignity in her bearing. She stopped in front of Sean and looked into his eyes.

"You're hurt," she said, raising her hand to his wound.

"It's nothing."

"I've never seen anyone fight like that before. Those men could have killed you with that club. My name is Lupe."

"I'm Sean McBride."

"That wound is going to need some attention. My house is nearby; come with me and I can bandage it for you."

"I'd like that."

The house was small and dark, with a brown wooden fence around it.

Lupe led Sean through the living room and into the kitchen, where they sat down at the dinner table. She poured some hot water in a pan and dropped a bar of soap and a washcloth in it. She washed the cut. Her touch was gentle and soothing. Yet being close to her reminded Sean of how lonely he really was.

"Where are you from?" Lupe asked.

"I was born in Ohio."

"Where did you learn to fight like that?"

"Vietnam."

Lupe dropped her towel and sprang to her feet. She stood there for a moment staring away. Then she started to cry.

Sean stood up, uncertain. "Did I say something wrong?"

"No," Lupe said, weeping. "It's my brother; he was killed in Vietnam."

Sean placed his hand on her shoulder. "I'm sorry; I didn't mean—"

"It's not your fault."

Lupe went into the bathroom and closed the door. Sean was thinking he should leave. This woman had been kind to him, and now she was upset. It was getting dark and he needed to find a place to camp anyway. Lupe returned.

"I should be going," Sean said.

"No, please stay. I'd like to talk to you."

"All right."

Lupe lit two candles and poured some red wine into glasses.

"He never talked about it," she said, handing Sean the wine. "My brother didn't talk about Vietnam in his letters. What was it like over there?"

Sean wanted to tell her what it had really been like in Vietnam, but he couldn't find the words. How could he describe the terror and the filth? The death, carnage, and insanity that he had experienced in one short year? What words could he possibly use to convey the loneliness and emptiness? How would he explain the fear he felt, waiting in a foxhole in the jungle for the enemy attack to come?

"It wasn't that bad," Sean said.

Lupe studied his face for a moment.

"I'm going to change; I'll be right back," she said, touching him on the back as she left.

Sean was beginning to relax. Lupe was a beautiful young woman. It felt good to be with her. On the other hand, being with a woman reminded him of what it was like to feel. In Vietnam, he had learned to shut out feelings. There had been too much pain there, too much insanity. To feel again meant he would have to confront the sadness and pain he carried deep within. Lupe was everything he was not. She was kind, gentle, open, and warm, the essence of life itself. He had walked with death. Tracking and killing men had been his trade. He was hardened and cynical at nineteen.

Lupe returned wearing a beige peasant dress, cut low at the neck. She had put on clear lipstick and changed her earrings to gold ones with white pearl tips. She sat down.

"You have sad eyes," Lupe said.

"Tell me about your brother."

"Thomas was eighteen when he joined the army. He was macho and very patriotic. He believed in this country. Our father fought in World War II. My uncle died in Korea. Thomas couldn't wait to go into the army. He had been in Vietnam eleven months when he was killed."

"I'm sorry."

"I don't understand any of it. He was so young. Sean, tell me what it was really like over there."

He stared away for a moment, remembering.

"I was scared the entire time I was there. I lost some good friends. The war changed my life forever. After a time, the killing and bloodshed seemed senseless. I think war is a crime. If you don't believe me, ask the infantry; ask the dead."

Sean was shaking. Lupe put her arms around him.

"Come and sit in the living room. I'll light a fire."

She lit a fire in the fireplace and brought him some brandy.

Sean sat in a rocking chair and watched the fire. He was beginning to feel alive for the first time in over a year. He walked over and studied the volumes in the bookcase. There was Hemingway, Steinbeck, Tolstoy, Dostoyevski, and Flaubert. Sean had always loved books. He understood that he was still a young man. His experience in war had shaped his thinking in unique ways. He knew he was different from other men. Sean had known hunger, thirst, fear, and death at a very early age. He had comported himself well. Lupe came into the room and sat down on the couch next to him.

"I haven't told you how lovely you look," he said. "When I look at you, I am reminded of a poem:

" 'Here with a little bread beneath the bough, a flask of wine, a book of verse and thou, beside me singing in the wilderness— Oh wilderness were paradise enow!'"

"That's beautiful."

The young couple talked into the night. Sean savored the time. Lupe looked so beautiful. Her lips were red from the wine, full and moist. The light from the fire danced in her eyes. She threw her head back and laughed at something he said.

"Will you stay with me tonight?" she asked.

"Yes."

Sean was already awake when the rooster began to crow. He had not slept. There were too many thoughts running through his mind. He had held Lupe in his arms after she fell asleep and watched her chest rise and fall. The first rays of morning light filtered through the curtains. Sean put on his trousers and went outside. The air was crisp and clear. He picked some wildflowers and took them inside. Lupe was awake.

"Good morning."

"Oh, flowers. Would you like some breakfast?"

"I sure would."

"Where will you go now?" she asked over breakfast.

"I don't know."

"Come back," she said.

When breakfast was over, Lupe walked Sean to his motorcycle. He kissed her on the lips, got on his bike, and rode away.

Chapter XII

Sean traveled for several months, but he was not finding the answers he sought. He decided to get a job. The man at the employment office told him there were no jobs available for someone with Sean's infantry skills. There were no hills to take, men to lead, or battles to fight. The state employee who had been sitting in a nice safe office while Sean had been at war was telling him he was unemployable. Sean McBride had risked everything for his country, shed his blood, and been willing to die if necessary. Now the nation was turning its back on him. Okay, if they wouldn't let him work, he would go to school.

At the university, Sean found that many of his friends from high school were about to graduate. On campus, *Vietnam* was a bad word. Four students had just been shot at Kent State University in Ohio during a war protest. Some Vietnam veterans were being misdiagnosed as schizophrenic by incompetent doctors and thrown into rat-infested Veterans Administration hospitals. When a friend introduced Sean as a Vietnam veteran at a campus party, he was met with silent stares. Wherever Sean went, people were asking him what it felt like to kill someone. Sean was having nightmares. He was getting anxious and depressed. People were openly ridiculing the returning veterans, calling them fools. The politicians, generals, and American people in general avoided responsibility for the war. The veterans themselves were made the scapegoats. Many killed themselves.

Sean was hurt and confused. He went to talk to a counselor on campus. She was an attractive psychiatrist, about thirty-five, well dressed.

"How can I help you?" she asked.

"I'm a Vietnam veteran. I've been feeling depressed, anxious," Sean said. "I've had some thoughts of suicide."

"I won't help you. You fought on the wrong side."

Sean left the office. He walked around for several hours, thinking. He understood now. There would be no help from his country. He had only himself, his family, and his Vietnam veteran brothers. They would have to help each other.

The gnawing pangs of hunger ripped through his guts like a bayonet. Sean McBride was no stranger to the feeling. In Vietnam, he had fought for days with little food or water, taking casualties all the while. His money was gone. He had not eaten today. The sandwich he was saving felt good and warm in his jacket pocket. He would find a nice, sunny spot and enjoy the food. That's when he saw the veteran. He was coming down the street, wearing an old army field jacket. He looked about Sean's age, but he was dirty, disheveled, and foraging through the garbage cans. The veteran found a piece of food and plopped it into his mouth. Sean walked over and touched the veteran's arm. The young man turned around. The light was gone from his eyes. He had the thousand-yard stare. Sean gave the veteran his sandwich. The vet sat down on a bench and devoured it quickly. Sean sat down beside him. The two Vietnam veterans sat quietly, not speaking but knowing. Sean gave his fallen brother a hug, and then they cried.

About the Author

MICHAEL MCCORMICK, who grew up in Jackson, Ohio, based the story told in *Across the Pond* on his own personal experiences as a U.S. Marine serving in Vietnam. Upon his return to the States in 1969, he was awarded the Purple Heart and the Silver Star. Since that time he has gone on to earn his B.A. and his M.A. in clinical psychology at John F. Kennedy University in Orinda, California. He now works as a psychotherapist, in which capacity he has actively worked with other Vietnam War veterans.

If you enjoyed reading this book please leave a star-rating and feedback on the author's **www.obooko.com** download page.

20057551R00032

Made in the USA
San Bernardino, CA
26 March 2015